Survival at Big Shark Key

by Dorothy Francis

Cover Illustration: Paul Lackner
Inside Illustration: Pat Muchmore

For Evelyn Gardner

PB ISBN-10: 0-7891-5098-0 ISBN-13: 978-0-7891-5098-1
RLB ISBN-10: 0-7807-9066-9 ISBN-13: 978-0-7807-9066-7
Printed in the U.S.A.
10 11 12 13 14 PP 15 14 13 12 11

400583621

Contents

1

Making Lists and Decisions

"Grady?"

Grady ignored the call. Just because Maggie was three years older, she thought she was the boss. A humid breeze floated through his window. He heard it swish the palm leaves outside.

"Grady, come on," Maggie said. "We're waiting."

Grady brushed his brown hair off his forehead. He stretched to thumbtack the picture of Charles Atlas, famous bodybuilder, to his wall. Next to Atlas was Franklin Roosevelt, famous president. Below the president was Charles Lindbergh, famous aviator.

Grady collected pictures of brave and famous men. Someday he planned to be brave and famous too. The pictures helped remind him of his goal.

A 1935 calendar hung on another wall. Beside it was his gold-framed spelling bee award. He had won that last week. The last day of school.

"Grady! Dad says right now. It's family forum time," Maggie said.

"Rats! I hate family forums," Grady said. He scowled at his skinny sister. But he laid the thumbtacks on his dresser. "Family forums mean trouble, Maggie. Last week we decided to substitute cornmeal mush for meat. Before that we agreed to skip movies. Rats to family forums."

Once seated at their round kitchen table, everyone looked at Dad. Tall and slender. Handsome. Grady hoped to look like Dad someday. Now Dad was still wearing his business suit and his tie with the diamond stickpin. Grady smelled his mother's Yankee Clover perfume. He eyed the pale yellow dress that matched her hair.

Dad cleared his throat. He said, "Well, I have some bad news. Mr. Baxter plans to do his own bookkeeping. So I've been fired." He sighed. "The recession has hit us."

"Oh, Frank." Mom ran to his side. She took his hand.

"Golly, Dad," Grady said. "Why you?"

"Why not me?" Dad asked. "Everyone's hurt by this recession. We're luckier than most. We have some choices. So let's discuss them. We can go on welfare while I hunt for work. We can live with my parents," Dad said. He paused before he continued. "Or we can move to Big Shark Key."

"No welfare, Frank," Mom said. "And we'd crowd your parents."

"Big Shark Key!" Grady exclaimed. "Where's that?"

"Mr. Baxter owns a deserted island in the Keys," Dad said. "There's a sturdy house on it. Mr. Baxter wants someone to live there."

"Why?" Mom asked. "Will he pay us?"

"Mr. Baxter wants to prevent Big Shark Key from becoming a smuggler's nest. That's less likely to happen if someone lives there," Dad explained.

"Sounds scary," Grady said.

"You're always afraid," Maggie said.

Grady didn't argue. Last month he had climbed too

high in a tree. Firemen had to rescue him. Yesterday Maggie had to save him from a riptide. Now he was afraid of the sea. And he was afraid of Big Shark Key.

"What would we live on?" Mom asked. "Fresh air and sunshine?"

"We'll catch seafood," Dad said. "There are orange trees and a lime grove. If we clear the grove, Mr. Baxter will buy the limes."

"What's a lime worth?" Maggie asked.

"One cent," Dad said.

"It'd take a lot of limes to amount to much," Grady said.

"I'm not forcing this," Dad stood. "I can go alone. The rest of you can stay with my folks."

"Frank, if you go, I go," Mom said.

"Me too," Maggie said. "It sounds exciting."

Grady squirmed. "I need to think it over. Please?" His stomach felt like a fist.

"Sure," Dad said. "Oh, there's one more thing. An old Conch and his son live on a sailboat near Big Shark Key. They fish for sponges."

"I thought a conch was a shellfish," Maggie said.

"Conch." Grady repeated the word. "It sounds like a conk on the head."

"Conch is a nickname for a person born on Key West," Dad said, smiling. "This Conch's name is Jeb Burltee. Hank is his son. He's about your age, Grady."

Grady gulped.

"Grady's such a goup," Maggie said. "He's scared again."

"Now, Maggie," Dad said. "Grady's as brave as anyone. You think on it, Grady. And remember the president's words. 'All we have to fear is fear itself.' We'll discuss this again tomorrow."

Grady ran to his room for pencil and paper. Then he walked to the porch. Hibiscus bushes circled the porch like a fence protecting him. He divided his paper into two columns: GO and STAY.

Under the GO column he wrote:	Under the STAY column he wrote:
Keep family together. Exciting adventure.	Like to live at Gramp's house. Hate leaving my friends. Hate bugs, roaches, ants, sand flies, mosquitoes. Hate rats and sea turtles. Hate stingrays and eels and fire ants. Smugglers?

He was still writing when Maggie appeared. "Making another crazy list?" she asked.

"They're not crazy," Grady said. "Lists help me think." He yelled when Maggie grabbed his list and read it. Anger boiled inside him like hot soup when she laughed.

"What's so funny, skinnybones?" he asked.

"You are, dingy." Maggie pointed to the list. "You're afraid of all those 'hate' things."

"Am not!" Grady yelled. But he knew Maggie was right. Maybe he was a coward. That was his worst fear.

The thought of a long boat ride made him sick. He stared at the floor. Then he looked up.

"Doesn't the sea ever scare you, Maggie?" he asked.

"Sometimes," Maggie confessed. She looked at Grady with a serious face. "I was scared when I rescued you from the riptide."

"You were? Does that make you a coward?" Grady asked.

"Of course not," Maggie snapped. "I'm a heroine. I acted in spite of my fear. I put on a brave look to fool people."

"Maybe I should practice looking brave," said Grady.

Maggie laughed. "You need a lot of practice. But it might work. If you fool others, you might fool yourself too."

Maggie looked at the concern in Grady's face. For a moment she felt sorry for him. "Grady, I want you to go," Maggie said. "We're a family. I'd miss you. But don't you dare tell anyone I said that." She quickly turned and went inside.

Grady picked up his list. Under GO he added, *Maggie wants me to go.* He scratched out the STAY column. Dad had called him brave, hadn't he? So he'd have to act brave. Grady ran to his room. Standing before his mirror, he practiced his brave look.

It took the family a week to pack. They stored furniture. They bought supplies. They traded Gramp their Ford for his powerboat. Grady hated it all. But he didn't complain.

Maggie might change her mind about wanting him along. And having Maggie's approval was like wearing a golden halo. Nobody could see it. But Grady knew it was there.

"Everyone can take one small suitcase," Dad said. "We'll wear swimsuits on the trip. Pack dungarees, tennis shoes, socks, and indoor slippers."

"Let's each take one unnecessary thing," Mom said. "I'm taking silver napkin rings. We may have to use bandanna handkerchiefs for napkins. But they'll be in elegant rings."

"I'm taking the fan Gram gave me," Maggie said. "Will there be a wall to hang it on?"

"I'm taking my spelling award," Grady said. So what if the others laughed? The award reminded him of one time when he had been brave. It had been scary standing before all his teachers, classmates, and those judges. But he had done it. "Dad, what are you taking?" he asked.

"My diamond stickpin," Dad said. "But it's not so unnecessary. If worse comes to worst, we can sell it. It could help us buy food."

"Frank!" Mom exclaimed. "We'll never sell your grandfather's stickpin. Why, it's a family heirloom."

"Worse things have happened than selling an heirloom," Dad said.

Grady was glad when Gramp arrived. He came to drive them to the dock. Grady loved Gramp. Thick white hair. Sea-blue eyes. Straight posture. He reminded Grady of a general reviewing his troops. Maybe he should have stayed with Gramp and Gram.

"Your gram's waiting at the dock with a surprise for you," Gramp told the family.

"Cookies for the trip?" Maggie asked.

But Gramp didn't tell. They all piled into the car and drove to the dock. Grady saw Gram first. Wide-brimmed straw hat. Blue dress. She looked like a sentinel guarding their boat. Or was she guarding that slatted crate nearby?

"Gram! Gram!" Maggie rushed to give her a hug.

Grady allowed Gram a kiss on the forehead. Then he knelt and peered inside the crate. "Gram! It's a . . . a goat! What will we do with a goat?" he asked.

"You'll milk it," Gram said. "I'll not have your teeth rotting from lack of milk."

"We'll drink goat's milk?" Maggie asked. "We may not like it."

"We'll learn to like it," Dad said. "And we'll learn to milk it. All of us."

"Your time on Big Shark Key will be a time of discovery," Gramp said. "Make the most of it—goat milk and all."

Grady gulped. Maybe they could train the critter to be a guard goat. He knew they'd need protection. But he kept the guard goat thought to himself. No point in Maggie knowing his fears.

Grady lifted his chin. He squared his shoulders. Then he squinted just a bit. That was the brave look he had practiced.

Would it work?

2
Home Sweet Home

Their blue boat had a banana painted on the stern. *The Banana Boat.* It took over an hour to load up. The boat rocked like a bathtub toy and thumped the dock.

As it came time to leave, Grady pulled on a sweatshirt in spite of the heat. Ocean breezes could make a guy shiver. Or were his shivers due to fear? He corked that thought.

Gram wiped her eyes. She kissed everyone for the third time. When Gramp blew his nose, it sounded like a foghorn. Grady felt as if a coconut had lodged in his throat. He could hardly shout good-bye as Dad started the motor. His arm felt heavy as an anchor as he waved.

A minute ago he could have changed his mind. But not now. Green sea lapped between *The Banana Boat* and the dock. They were off.

The weatherman had promised calm seas. But waves knocked Grady sideways. Spray wet his sweatshirt and his hair. The bigness of the sea scared him. Or was it his own smallness he found so scary?

"Hawk Channel to our right," Dad shouted.

"What's Hawk Channel?" Grady asked. "A special place where osprey fly?"

"No, silly," Maggie said. "It's a deep channel running between the land and the Gulf Stream."

Bossy, know-it-all Maggie! He was sorry he had asked.

"How much farther, Mom?" Grady asked after an hour.

"How should I know?" Mom shrugged. "I've never been out here before. Ask your dad."

But he didn't ask. Instead, he let his back curve forward. He rested his head on his knees. And he closed his eyes until Maggie shouted.

"We're here!" she yelled. "Hello, Big Shark Key! Wake up, Grady. We're here at last."

Grady looked up. His heart was pounding. His throat began to close until he gasped for air.

"Mom! Big Shark Key! It's a jungle!" Grady cried. He eyed the tangled mass of low-growing trees. Their roots arched above the water like dark snakes.

"Mangroves," Dad said. "People call them 'island builders.' They drop seeds into the water. Then shoots sprout. They grow farther and farther into the sea."

"The dock," Grady wailed. "It doesn't even reach the shore." But he saw a small beach and a sunken skiff half-buried in sand. "How will we get our stuff to shore?"

Dad eased the boat to the dock. "Tie us up, Grady," he said.

Grady tied the stern line to a dock cleat. He used a half hitch he had learned in Boy Scouts.

"All right!" Maggie shouted as Grady finished his knot. "Didn't think you could do it."

For a moment Grady felt proud of his success. Maybe he could cope with Big Shark Key. He looked into the water. It looked just a foot or two deep. Removing his sweatshirt, he stood. He held his nose and jumped overboard.

Grady splashed into the clear water. His head went under, and then he bobbed up. The water came up to his shoulders. It was deeper than he had thought.

He felt like he had just jumped into a swimming pool. But then he remembered that he was standing in an ocean. What was lurking underneath the water, ready to bite his toes? Or munch on his leg for lunch? He drew in a quick breath and accidentally swallowed some water. He began coughing and spluttering. Maggie laughed.

"Are you okay?" Mom stretched a hand to him, leaning over the gunwale.

"Sure. The water's great," Grady said. In spite of his fear, he put on his brave look.

Maggie jumped in too. "Hand us some things, Dad. We'll wade them to shore."

"What about the goat?" Grady asked. "Do goats swim?"

"Who knows?" Mom asked with a laugh. "We'd better carry it to shore."

"It'll take all of us to heft that crate," Dad said.

Dad jumped in first. Then Mom handed Dad, Maggie, and Grady the crate. Mom jumped in to help. They tried to keep the goat's head above the water. It began to kick its legs inside the crate as the family waded it to shore. Goats must be scared of the ocean too, Grady thought.

The family got the goat to the shore. Then Maggie

opened the crate. The goat ran into the thicket like a cork popping from a bottle.

Grady looked around the island. "Where's the house?" he asked.

"Let's follow this trail," Dad said. He led off, pushing through weeds and coral rock.

When at last they saw the house, Grady stared. Gulls screamed. Two turkey vultures flew up from the mangroves. The house sat low to the ground. Grady eyed the shed out back. Had he really expected an indoor bathroom? One with running water? He hoped the dark shutters on the house hid lots of windows.

Dad unlocked the door with a skinny black key. Grady thought he heard the scurry of feet. But he saw nothing. Maggie wrinkled her nose. "Smells like that pirate's chest at the museum," she said.

Using his toe, Grady wrote his name in the dust on the floor. "Home sweet home."

A pine wall about four feet high divided the house lengthwise. Muslin curtains drooped from the ceiling to the pine divider. Five doorways opened into tiny bedrooms. The only furniture—faded mattresses on rusty bedsprings.

"Grady," Dad said. "Open the shutters. Maggie, clear some of that coral rock from the path. We've lots to do before dark."

Grady hated thinking about dark. What if he felt something crawling in his bed?

"Hey!" Maggie shouted. "The goat's back."

"She needs to be milked," Mom said.

"I'll try," Dad said. He worked hard before the milk flowed. But he filled half a pail.

"Who wants first taste?" Mom asked.

Nobody spoke.

"We'll all try it together," Mom said. She passed out cups. On the count of three, they drank.

The milk had a sweetish taste. It felt thick. And it smelled like—goat.

"Perhaps we'll learn to drink it," Mom said. Grady smiled at her for not insisting that she liked it.

Dad built an outdoor fire. They roasted hot dogs and potatoes. They picked and ate oranges for dessert. Maggie placed their few dirty dishes in a roasting pan.

"I cleared the table," she said. She handed the roaster to Grady like a gift. "Your turn to wash."

Grady peered at the messy dishes. Ants had moved onto them. Roaches were arriving. But Grady used his brave look instead of making a fuss.

"Wash them in the sea tonight," Mom said. "We'll set up a better system tomorrow."

Grady carried the dishes to the beach and waded into the water. A good way to do dishes, he thought. Pitch them into the sea. Then he jumped as something bumped his legs. Small fish swarmed in. They slurped the ants and roaches.

"Rinse them again in fresh water," Mom said when

he returned to the house. "There's a cistern. We'll have fresh water as long as we get some rain."

"How does water get into the cistern?" Grady asked.

"It drains into pipes on the roof," Dad explained.

"We're going to drink dirty roof water!" Grady felt his stomach churn.

"Dirt filters out as the water stands in the tank," Dad said. "You'll get used to it. Cistern water is the only fresh water in the Keys."

Dad had already put their cake of ice in the icebox. Mom placed leftover hot dogs on top of it.

"Tomorrow we'll treasure hunt for things we need. Like jars and lids," Dad said.

"Did pirates come ashore here?" Grady asked.

"Not that I know of," Dad said. "But ship passengers throw things overboard. We'll find jars. And maybe some lumber too."

That night they left their personal items in their suitcases. But Grady placed his spelling award on an empty bed. He wondered if mosquito netting would keep out roaches too. They sat in the kitchen talking until Maggie pointed to the ceiling.

"A rat, Dad. A rat!" she shouted.

"Good thing we brought poison," Dad said. "Go into the other room, and I'll set it out." Grady ran to his room and threw himself on the bed.

How could he stand living here with roaches and rats? Grady didn't even bother to change into pajamas. He hated Big Shark Key. He hated it a lot. And he hated it because he was afraid. Because he was a coward.

He lay thinking for a long time. He was just dozing off when he heard someone singing. Or was it his imagination? Nobody would be singing on this horrible island.

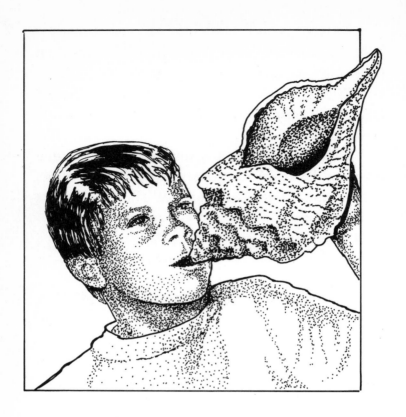

3
The Demijohn Thief

Where am I? Grady wakened, full of panic. Then he remembered. Big Shark Key. Jungle. Rats. Putting on his brave look, he joined the family for breakfast in the kitchen.

"About time, Grady," Maggie said. "We're on floor-scrubbing duty."

"I'll cut weeds," Dad said. "When the floor's clean, we'll unpack suitcases."

After breakfast Dad tossed sand on the floor. Then he sloshed on seawater and handed his children brooms. "Sweep the sand out the door. It's a method I learned the hard way—in the army."

It took sweat and muscle. But after a long time the floor was clean. The family spent the rest of the morning unpacking their meager supplies before eating lunch.

The family rested for a few minutes before they planned their afternoon. Then Dad said, "Time to treasure hunt. But first I'll show you our telephones." He put a conch shell to his mouth. Then he blew on it.

"Weird," Grady said. "It sounds like a ghost."

"I found the empty shells at the beach," Dad said. "I hacked off the ends with my machete. Smoothed them down with sand. Each shell's a different size. So each has a different sound. We can identify one another by pitch." They blew and laughed. They continued practicing until everyone could get a loud tone.

"Grady, make a list," Dad said.

Grady beamed as nobody poked fun at his list making. He found pencil and paper.

"Put 'easy chair' on the list," Mom said. "And a footstool."

"Dream on, Anna," Dad laughed. "But we might find lumber. Grady, start the list with 'lumber.' Then 'sealed cans.' Next, write 'demijohns.' "

"What's that?" Grady asked as he attempted to spell it. He pretended like it was the spelling bee he had won.

"Demijohns are bottles. They're about a gallon in size. And they're usually enclosed in wicker," Dad explained.

"Weird name for a bottle," Grady said.

Dad continued the list. "Write 'coconuts.' And anything else that looks interesting. I'll sound my conch horn every half hour. Return my signal so I'll know you're okay. Stash your finds above the high tide line. We'll pick them up later."

Grady stayed with Maggie. Beach walking was easy. But he stumbled when they reached the mangrove roots.

"Hey!" Grady shouted. "A coconut." He waded to it. Then he tossed it ashore.

"Demijohn!" Maggie pulled up a green bottle laced in wicker.

When Maggie and Grady heard Dad's conch horn, they blew replies. "Some telephone," Grady said. But he liked knowing Dad was near. They found more bottles, sealed cans, and a piece of lumber.

"Let's head back," Grady said. "We can't carry all

this stuff." He didn't admit he was afraid to go farther from the house.

They splashed from the sea into the jungle. Branches scratched them as they dragged boards behind them.

"We left our demijohn along here somewhere," Maggie said.

They struggled a while longer. Then Grady poked Maggie. He pointed at someone about 200 feet away. "Look. Someone's stealing our bottle!"

"Hey there!" Maggie started to chase the thief. But she tripped over a mangrove root. "Go after him, Grady. That demijohn's ours."

"He's too fast," Grady said, silently excusing his fear.

"Stop!" Maggie shouted.

The boy kept running. Clearly, he knew secret paths. Grady watched until the boy disappeared. Dark hair. Blue shirt and dungarees. Ankle boots.

"Must be Hank Burltee," Grady said. "Some friend he's going to be. A common thief!"

"Hank!" Maggie called. "Hank Burltee! Come back."

In seconds the boy had disappeared like a ghost. Had they really seen him? Grady shivered. He squinted into the thicket until his eyes watered. Silence. He and Maggie stood gawking—and alone.

"It had to be Hank Burltee," Maggie said. "He knew that bottle was ours. I think he was spying on us."

Grady thought about the singing he had heard the night before. Maybe Hank Burltee had been hiding—watching. "Maybe he thinks we're the spies. Maybe he doesn't want us on his island," Grady said.

They heard a blast from Dad's conch horn. Grady was relieved as they walked toward the sound. When they met their parents, they told them what had happened.

"Let's forget it," Dad said. "We'll be meeting the Burltees soon. I want us to be friends."

"We'll find more bottles," Mom said.

Dad husked their coconut and laid it aside. Using a scallop shell, he pried the lid from a can. "Tar," he said.

"Smells like the stuff they spread on our street at home," Grady said.

"Right," Dad said. "A great find. We'll raise that sunken skiff. Maybe we can mend it with this tar."

"Mom!" Grady said. "You found a board for your chair."

Mom laughed. "Or maybe a plank to connect the dock and shore."

Grady sifted sand through his fingers. "Think we might find a gold doubloon buried here? At school we read about Spanish galleons sinking in the Keys. They carried gold and silver from the New World back to Spain."

"You might find gold," Dad said. "If divers could salvage those lost ships, the riches might end the Depression."

"Why doesn't someone do that?" Grady asked.

"Divers can't stay underwater long enough," Dad said. "Maybe someday."

They rested. Then Dad and Grady fished for their supper. They kept only two big yellowtails. Mom drained milk from the coconut and made a pudding.

Later Dad called the meal "a banquet." Grady called the pudding—"different." Even Goat liked the fish.

"Grady," Mom said. "I want you to keep a journal. A diary. In future years it will remind us of this time. And make a calendar. Mark off each day with an *X.*"

Grady wondered who would want to be reminded of fear and thieves. But he began a journal. He liked to write. And he liked to write something besides lists. The following week passed quickly. Grady *X*-ed each day on his calendar.

With much hard work, the family raised the skiff. Little by little they scraped off barnacles. They would scour small areas with sand. Then they would rest and cool off.

Before long the skiff was seaworthy. Dad and Maggie rowed it in the shallows around the island.

One day Dad made an announcement. "Today we're going to the lime grove and clear weeds. If there's time, we'll pick a few limes. I've found the grove and cleared a trail."

"We're lucky limes are a year-round crop," Mom said. "We'll earn a little money in spite of these hard times."

Grady wore dungarees and a shirt. Lime trees had thorns.

He hid his disappointment when they reached the grove. He could hardly see the trees for the weeds and vines. Dad swung the scythe. Mom hacked at the thicket with a machete. Grady and Maggie pulled vines from the branches. They were like living ropes.

While they were resting, Grady felt hairs rise on the back of his neck. Was someone watching them? He studied the thicket.

"Look, Maggie," Grady whispered. "See? The kid with the dark hair."

Maggie saw him and shouted, "Hey there! We want to talk to you."

Grady expected the boy to run. But he didn't. Now what? They were about to meet a thief, eyeball to eyeball.

4

Bird Drawings and a Birthing Shell

Grady and Maggie approached the boy slowly.

"Who are you?" the boy called to them.

Grady forced himself to step forward. "I'm Grady Cummings. And this is my sister, Maggie."

"I'm Hank." The boy's voice sounded low and reedy.

"We're glad to meet you," Grady said, "but we want to know why you stole our demijohn."

"Didn't steal it. Just borrowed it for a spell," he said.

"So bring it back," Grady said. "Next time, ask before you borrow."

"Don't be a mope," Hank said. "I'm not afraid of you. If you want the bottle, come borrow it back."

Mope? Was this kid calling him a dummy? *Mope* must be Key West Conch talk.

"The bottle's on our sailboat in Hidden Cove," Hank taunted.

What was going on here? Did Hank think he could keep the demijohn because they were afraid to come get it? Grady practiced his brave look.

"Take me to your sailboat," Grady said. "How far is it?"

Hank laughed. "Best do your borrowing when nobody's home."

"That would be stealing," Grady said. "I'm no thief."

"Bet I can hold my breath longer than you can," Hank said.

Grady blinked at the sudden change of subject. Hank scared him. Hank made him mad. But he couldn't resist being his audience. "Okay. How long can you hold your breath?" he asked.

"One minute and a half," Hank said proudly.

"Bet you can't," Grady said. He showed Hank his watch with a second hand.

Hank took a deep breath. Grady and Maggie watched the second hand. Sure enough! Hank held his breath over 90 seconds.

"How'd you learn to do that?" Grady asked, impressed.

"From Pap. He spots a sponge. I dive to see if it's the right size before he hooks it up. I stay underwater a long time," Hank said.

"Grady can bend his thumb back until it touches his wrist," Maggie said. "Bet you can't do that."

Grady did his thumb trick. Hank tried and failed. He looked at Grady with new respect. Grady wondered if Hank still thought he was a mope.

Hank changed the subject. "You want your bottle back, come home with me. I'll get it for you. We'll take my skiff."

Maggie walked toward her mother. She left Grady to deal with Hank.

"You got a skiff of your own?" Grady asked.

"Sure do," Hank said. "Pap gave it to me when I turned eight. Come with me. I'll show you our sailboat."

"I'll have to ask my parents," Grady said.

"Mope."

"That isn't being a mope. My parents care about me. They need to know where I am and what I'm doing. If you can't wait until I ask, then I'm not going with you."

"So ask," Hank said. "Tell them you'll be safe."

Hank began humming, and Grady felt himself stiffen. He remembered the strange singing he had heard. Hank? Surely Hank had been spying. Maybe going to Hank's sailboat wasn't a safe thing to do. But he asked permission and received it. Dad wanted the two families to be friends.

"Ready to go?" Hank said. He led Grady to the water. His skiff bobbed like a giant fishing lure at the end of a line. It was fastened to a mangrove root. A pelican flew as they approached. Its wings made loud *flup-flup* sounds.

"*Prince Hank,* Key West, Florida." Grady read the words on the boat's stern. How great to have a boat named after you! Did Hank really think he was a prince?

"Get aboard," Hank ordered. "You sit aft. I'll sit amidships and row."

"Want me to help?"

"Don't be a mope," Hank said. "Bet you don't know how to row."

Grady kept his lack of rowing experience a secret. He'd learn first chance he had. "We have a skiff," Grady said.

"Bet you're lying," answered Hank.

"Am not," Grady argued. "Come to our house and see for yourself."

"I will. Count on it," Hank said.

Was that a threat or a promise? Grady wondered.

Sometimes waves made the rowing hard, but Hank didn't let on. He paused when a screaming gull swooped overhead.

"It's checking to see if we've got fish," Hank said. "Gulls are beggars. Who needs all their screaming!"

"I like them," Grady said.

"Don't be a mope. They're common. I like pelicans and cormorants."

Around the next bend, Grady saw the green sailboat. Its yellow sails hung limp. The main mast pointed skyward like a polished wooden finger.

"*The Neptune,* Key West, Florida." Grady read the boat's name. "How do you board without a dock?"

"Mope." Hank rowed to the sailboat. "We use that ladder."

Grady's chin dropped. His shoulders came unsquared. Did Hank actually expect him to climb that flapping rope?

"I'll go first," Hank offered.

Before Grady could argue, Hank pulled the skiff to the ladder. He cast the anchor and scrambled up the ropes.

What a fix! He couldn't sit forever in the skiff and let Hank call him a mope—again.

Inching forward, Grady leaned over the bow. He managed to catch the ladder. Rough hemp bit into his hands as he held it like a lifeline. He climbed. Surely it wasn't more than a dozen feet. But his stomach turned like a Ferris wheel. At last Hank grasped his hand and pulled him over the gunwale to the deck.

"You did swell for a first-timer," Hank said.

Grady recognized rare praise. Maybe they could be friends after all. He grabbed the railing to keep his footing. He looked around the boat. "It's really nice, Hank," he said. "Where do you sleep? Where do you keep your things?"

"Pap sleeps right on deck in a sleeping bag," Hank said. "I have a bunk below deck. Come on. I'll show you."

Grady followed Hank down narrow steps into a cramped cabin. It smelled of mildew. Built-in table. Bench. Stove. Bunk. There was little free space. Hank raised the bottom of his bunk, revealing room for storage.

Hank pulled out a box and opened it. "My shell collection," he said proudly. "Here's a scallop. And a volute. A cowry. Long ago cowries were used for

34

money. Pap drilled a hole in it so I can wear it around my neck."

"Did you find the shells around here?" Grady asked.

"No," Hank answered. "A reef near Hawk Channel keeps shells from washing up here. I bought these in Key West. Do you collect anything?"

Grady hesitated, feeling Hank getting the upper hand. Then he had an idea. Hank had bought his shells. Anybody could buy shells. Anybody. "Hank, I do collect something. Words," Grady said.

"Words?" Hank asked.

"Sure," Grady said. "I think of words, and then I write them into poems. Learned how at school. Sometime I'll let you read them."

"Sounds crazy to me. If you had a decent collection, maybe we could trade some things. But I'm not trading shells for words," said Hank.

Grady spotted a conch shell.

"That's my birthing shell," Hank said. "Key West people hang a conch shell in the yard to tell neighbors a baby's born. Mam gave me my birthing shell before she died."

Hank opened a blue folder of sketches. "Sometimes I draw pelicans and cormorants."

Grady felt bad about Hank's mom. "Hank, maybe we could work together and write our own book. I do words. You do pictures," Grady suggested.

"Might work—if your words are good enough," Hank added.

Grady choked back a sharp reply. He saw the edge of a sketch Hank tried to hide. "What's that one?" he asked.

Hank's face flushed. "I'm trying to sketch myself. I look into a mirror, then draw. Pap calls it my self-portrait," he said.

"I think it's pretty good," Grady said. "Did you learn to draw at school?"

"Naw. I learned on my own. Don't do much with school," he said.

"Don't truant officers get you?" Grady asked.

"Hard for them to find us," Hank said. He held up the demijohn. "Want your bottle back?"

5

Sponging for Black Blobs

Hank handed Grady the demijohn. Grady looped the wicker covering around his hand.

"Where's your father?" Grady asked.

"Out sponging," Hank said. He pointed to a dark speck on the horizon. "He'll be in soon. Once Pap met up with rumrunners. They were hiding from the Border Patrol. They made Pap hide their liquor under his sponge canvas. Then they pretended to be fishermen."

"Did they get caught?" Grady asked.

"Naw. Went scot-free," Hank said.

"Have you ever seen a rumrunner?" Grady asked.

"Sure," Hank replied.

"What do they look like?" Grady asked.

"Big. Shoulders like hams. Whiskers. Long hair. Raggedy clothes," Hank said. "You'd be purely scared if you ever met up with one."

Grady peered at the sea. Maybe a rumrunner was headed their way right this minute. He felt the hairs rise on the back of his neck again.

"Hank, I've gotta be going," Grady said.

"So go," Hank said. "I said I'd bring you here. Didn't mention taking you back."

Grady's shoulders almost slumped. Then he squared them. He didn't want Hank to know he was scared.

Grady tied the demijohn to his belt and crawled down the rope ladder. Could Hank tell he was shaking with fear when he splashed into the sea?

His wet clothes dragged like a canvas tent as he swam to shore. He and Hank would never be friends.

Grady blew on the conch. Soon Maggie came to get him. "Hank acts like a big shot, Maggie. He acts like he really thinks he's somebody," Grady complained.

"Guess everybody's somebody if they take time to figure out who. That's the hard part," Maggie said. "Tell me about the sailboat."

Grady grabbed the chance he saw opening for him. Maggie wanted to know about the sailboat. And he wanted to know about skiffs.

"Let me help row, Maggie. Please," Grady said. "I need to know how to use the skiff alone."

"So you can impress Hank?" Maggie asked.

"That wouldn't impress him. But it might keep him from calling me a mope," he said.

Maggie changed places with Grady. She showed him how to grip the oars and pull on them. Then lift for the next dip and pull. To Grady's surprise, it wasn't that hard. He told Maggie about the sailboat as he rowed.

"It's smelly as an old sock. And the rigging creaks and groans. I feel sorry for Hank having to live there," Grady said.

"He probably feels sorry for you living in a shack and drinking goat's milk," Maggie replied.

Grady was too tired to talk anymore. Once at home, he told his folks about his visit with Hank. Then he ate and went to bed.

The next morning Goat began bleating. And Grady heard a strange shout.

"Jeb Burltee says hallo to the Cummingses," the voice yelled.

Grady heard the cracking of underbrush first. Then he saw a dark, shaggy head and a tall man with shoulders like hams. He was wearing raggedy clothes. And he carried two demijohns in one hand as if they were pint bottles. Hank followed in his shadow.

"Good morning," Dad called. Hank nodded his greeting. Grady remembered Hank's description of a rumrunner. He had merely described his dad. He probably hadn't seen a rumrunner at all.

"We've come to borrow drinking water," Jeb Burltee said.

"Help yourself," Dad said.

As everyone approached the water tank, Grady waited for Hank to speak. Hank surely had seen their skiff. Would he apologize for calling him a liar?

Hank looked at the ground a few seconds. Then he pulled his cowry shell from his pocket. "Want to put it around your neck until we leave?" he asked Grady.

Grady reached for the shell. He knew it was Hank's substitute for an apology.

Grady pulled a poem from his pocket and gave it to Hank. "Here's something I wrote," he said. "You can read it. Then I want it back." Hank unfolded the paper and read aloud.

"Such a common bird!
Who wants a gull for a friend?
I do. That's who. Me."

"It's a haiku," Grady explained. "First line has five syllables. Second line has seven syllables. Third line has five syllables. Those are the writing rules."

"Doesn't rhyme," Hank said. "Not real poetry like Mam used to read me."

"Boy," Mr. Burltee said to Grady, "want to come sponging with us? Promises to be a great day on the water."

Grady stalled. Did he want to go with a man who looked like a rumrunner? With a boy who called him a mope?

"It'd be a great experience," Dad said.

"Nothing to be scared of," Hank said. Then he winked. It was like a dare.

Grady gulped. Then he put on his brave face. "Sure, I'd like to go," he said. He invited Hank inside while he changed into his swimsuit.

"That's one purely pretty picture," Hank said. He was eyeing Grady's spelling bee award. "I'll trade you my self-portrait for it. When I finish it."

"Don't want to trade. That award's important," Grady said. He liked Hank's self-portrait. And he wished Hank would offer to trade it for something else, but he didn't.

Grady said good-bye to the family. Then he followed the Burltees aboard their skiff. Jeb motored along the light green water near the shoreline. On past *The Neptune*. Then into the deep blue water near the channel. When he cut the motor, the sea grew still as a whisper.

"That's the hook pole," Hank explained. Jeb was lifting a three-pronged pole and peering into the sea. "When Pap sees a sponge below, he'll pull it up with that pole."

"Hank," Jeb said. "Dive in and measure this first one."

Grady peered into the water. He saw nothing unusual except some giant black warts on the side of a rock. Hank grabbed a metal measuring ring and dove. Grady tasted salt from the splash Hank made. He leaned to watch as Hank followed Jeb's pole. Once in position, Hank tried to fit the ring over the black blob of sponge.

The ring wouldn't fit. Hank motioned to Jeb. And Jeb placed the pole prongs under the sponge. He pulled it up. Hank swam up too. Then he climbed back into the boat.

Grady eyed the black blob. It didn't look like a sponge to him.

"Do you measure each one?" Grady asked.

"Naw. Just the ones that might be too small to sell," Hank said. "We let those grow a while. Get 'em next year."

Jeb brought up dozens of sponges. Then he laid his pole aside. "I'll take you two to the corral. Then you can begin cleaning these critters."

"A sea corral?" Grady asked.

"Sure," Hank said. "Pap made it himself."

They motored to a circle of stakes sticking above the surface and held in place with a hemp line. It looked like a swimming area marked off for safety.

"We'll get inside it. Then I'll show you how to clean a sponge," Hank said. "Follow me. The water's shallow here."

They splashed into the corral. Then Jeb handed Hank a paddle. It looked like a Ping-Pong paddle with holes in it.

"How do we get out of here?" Grady asked. He felt trapped.

"Just push on the stakes," Hank said. "They'll give enough to let you swim over the top. But right now we're here to clean sponges."

Grady watched Hank pick up a sponge. He held it aloft. Then he hit it with the paddle. Its black skin broke away. Squishy matter oozed from it.

"Hank, I don't like this," Grady said.

"Scared of a little gurry?" Hank asked.

"No. I just hate being in the water with this awful sponge stuff," Grady said.

"If you want out, go over the side and wade to shore," Hank told him.

Grady paused. He hated for Hank to think he was a coward and a quitter. Before he could decide what to do, he screamed in spite of himself.

"What's the matter?" Hank shouted.

"Behind you!" Grady yelled. "A monster turtle. And it's heading right for us!"

6

Aliens in Canvas Bags

The sea churned as Hank turned. He was still holding the paddle. Grady felt as if the scene were playing in slow motion. The smell and taste of sea salt choked him. The turtle was as big as a card table. He watched it stick its ball-like head from its brown shell. Its eyes were like black marbles.

The monster swam toward them. All of a sudden Hank whacked it with his paddle. *Kerwham!* Grady knew he would always remember that sound.

The turtle submerged. Hank and Grady swam to safety.

"Scared us, didn't he?" Hank gasped for breath.

Grady had never been so scared. Maybe Hank had saved his life. Surely Hank was a hero. And just as surely, he, Grady, was a coward. He waited for Hank to call him a mope. But that didn't happen.

"That's enough for today," Hank said. "Climb into the skiff. I'll take you home."

Grady obeyed. "I'll help row," he said.

They each took an oar. To Grady's surprise, Hank began to sing.

"Oh when the saints . . . come marching in
Oh when the saints come marching in,
How I want to be in that number
When the saints come marching in."

Grady remembered the singing he had heard that first night on the island. Had it been Hank? Had Hank been spying on them?

"Nice song, Hank," Grady said.

"My mam sang it a lot. Mam came from Louisiana—a ways from here. Said she learned the song from her mam," Hank said.

"Hank, doesn't the sea ever scare you? I mean just a little bit?" Grady asked.

"No. You scared of it?" Hank asked.

Grady stalled. Did he really want to share his fear? What if Hank called him a mope—again?

"Hey," Hank said. "Answer me. You scared of the sea?"

"Sometimes," Grady admitted. "A lot of times, really. The sea makes me feel so little."

"You are little," Hank laughed. "We're both little. Little parts of a big world. But being little's no reason to be a mope."

At least Hank hadn't actually called him a mope. When they reached the dock, Grady climbed from the skiff. "Thanks, Hank."

Hank turned the skiff about. Then he called over his shoulder. "Grady?"

"What?" Grady answered.

"I don't admire gulls. But I liked your *high coo*. Maybe I'll sketch a gull for our book."

Grady grinned. Sometimes Hank was okay. "I'd like a sketch of a gull, Hank. And maybe I'll write a haiku about a pelican," he said.

Grady watched until his friend's skiff faded like mist into the distance. His friend. Grady liked the idea. Hank had saved them from the turtle. But Grady remembered that he had shouted the warning. Maybe he wasn't a coward after all. He had taken action in spite of his fear. Surely two people who had saved each other were bound to be friends.

Late that afternoon as Grady and Dad fished from the dock, a speedboat approached. "Ben!" Dad shouted. "Good to see you."

Grady relaxed. The man was Dad's friend.

"Been doing some sport fishing," Ben said. As he stepped on the dock, a slip of paper fluttered from his shirt pocket. Grady picked it up. But Ben snatched it from him. Grady had seen it was a list. He liked people who made lists.

Ben showed Dad the slip. "I'm picking up a load tonight. I need a hiding place if things get hot," he said.

What was this about? Grady walked off a little ways. He hoped the men would forget he was listening.

"Ben," Dad said. "Times are tough. But I want no part of rumrunning. Why are you carrying a liquor list? It's evidence. You'll get caught."

"I've already made some big money runs," Ben said. "I need the list to help me keep track of my order. If the law comes, I swallow the list and act like a fisherman. I could set you up in business, Frank."

"No thanks, Ben," Dad said. "You'll end up doing time in Atlanta."

Jail time, Grady wondered. Suddenly he didn't like Ben very much. Rumrunning! Grady could hardly believe it. Ben wasn't tall, shaggy, or raggedy. In fact, he looked a lot like Dad. A lot Hank knew about rumrunners!

Suddenly Ben snapped to attention. They heard another boat in the distance. Ben dropped into his speedboat. In moments he had disappeared through a cut between Big Shark Key and a nearby island.

Ben had only been gone a few minutes when another boat stopped at their dock. Grady's heart pounded. Was Ben out of sight? Was he safe? He didn't dare look.

"It's the Border Patrol," Dad said to Grady. "Let me do the talking."

"You going to tell on Ben?" Grady asked.

"I'll answer their questions honestly," Dad said.

The Border Patrol officers eased to the dock. Grady walked to meet his mother and Maggie, who had come to see the visitors.

"Welcome," Dad called. "Good to have company."

Grady listened to the introductions. The short, red-haired man was called Ace. His partner, Lucky, was bald and tall. He had a harmonica in his shirt pocket. Both men wore tan uniforms and carried holstered guns.

"How about some coffee?" Mom asked.

"Why not?" Ace said. "That guy in the red speedboat is slick as spit. We've lost him again. You didn't see that boat, did you?"

Dad smiled. "Matter of fact, Ben Martin stopped here a while ago. He's an old friend. We used to work for Baxter Pack in Miami," he said.

"What was he doing out here?" Lucky asked.

Grady held his breath. Friends didn't rat on friends. Honest men didn't lie.

"Said he was sportfishing," Dad said. "You might catch up with him if you know some shortcuts."

"Naw," Ace said. "He's too far ahead by now. We'll get him one of these days. He's just a rumrunner. It's the guys who run aliens that I can't stomach."

"Right," Lucky agreed. "They're would-be murderers."

Grady tried to turn his ears off. But Lucky's words seeped through. "Each alien pays for passage to America. Then he's stuffed into a weighted canvas bag with only his head showing. A drawstring for breathing room is tightened around his neck."

Ace took up the story. "If a patrol gives chase, the aliens are dumped overboard. They die. They leave no evidence."

Grady felt sick. How could such awful things happen right in the world where he lived! He was glad when Ace and Lucky left.

At supper his appetite left him. He spent a long time writing in his journal. Life was confusing! He hated to think of Ben the List Maker getting caught. He refused to think about aliens being dumped into the sea. Surely there was a fine line between right and wrong.

Before he put his journal away, he worked on another haiku. He scratched out words and added more. Sometimes he scratched out whole lines. Did Hank toss out lots of pelican pictures before he sketched a good one?

He read over the haiku that he decided to keep.

Bright-eyed pelican
Diving for dinner, do you
Ever miss your prey?

Would Hank like this haiku? Or would he read it and call him a mope?

7

The Brave Face

The days passed like pearls sliding from a string. Grady made Hank a horn from his birthing shell. In the afternoons they signaled each other. One blast said, "let's swim." Two blasts said, "let's go beachcombing."

Three blasts meant they would draw and write. Grady liked those times best.

But one day he accepted Hank's invitation to help string sponges. From the skiff, Hank pointed into the distance.

"There's Pap way out there. The gurry he beats from the sponges contains seeds that start new ones. Pap lets it fall where sponges like to grow. He says that's protecting our business," Hank said.

When they reached *The Neptune,* Hank scrambled up the ladder. Grady waited below. When Jeb pulled alongside the skiff, Grady tried not to stare at his wind-snarled hair and beard. If someone had told Grady to imagine a pirate, Jeb would have come to mind. He smelled the fishy odor around Jeb. It came from the sponges. Didn't it?

Hank skinned back down the ladder. He carried fishing line between his teeth. He clutched two long, big-eyed needles in one hand.

"Pap carved these needles from turtle shells," Hank said as he handed Grady a needle.

Jeb lashed the two skiffs together with a hemp line. Then he boarded the sailboat. "Shout when you're finished, Hank. And I'll haul the strings aboard," he said.

"Each line is four feet long," Hank said, threading the needles. "Thread a sponge on and tie a knot. Then add more sponges until there's just room to tie another knot."

Grady picked up a sponge. How he wanted to wipe the damp slick from his hands onto his jeans! But he didn't. He tied one sponge onto the line. When he picked up the second sponge, Hank stopped him.

"Not that one, Grady," Hank said. "You've started with a glove sponge. So thread the whole string with that kind. Makes 'em easier for Pap to sell at the auction house."

It took two hours to string the sponges. Grady's fingers ached. He felt like cheering when Hank shouted, "All finished, Pap."

Grady handed each string to Hank, who clung midway up the ladder. Hank handed them on to Jeb. When all the sponges were aboard the sailboat, Jeb climbed the rigging. He hung the strings high among the masts to dry.

With the job finished, Jeb and Hank rowed Grady home. They walked to the house. Mom and Dad met them at the door.

"Got a favor to ask," Jeb said. "Tomorrow I sail to Key West to the sponge auction. I'm asking if Hank could bunk here while I'm gone. It'll be a week or so."

"Hank's welcome, Jeb," Frank said, "but tomorrow Anna and I are taking our limes to market in Homestead. Not enough room for limes and passengers."

"Could we wait a week?" Anna asked.

"Afraid not," Frank said.

Frank turned to Jeb. "We're leaving Grady and Maggie here while we're gone. We'll be away a day, a night, part of another day."

Fear chilled Grady like a cold wind. He hadn't attended any family forums about being left alone overnight. What if . . . Grady looked at Maggie. She didn't look scared. Why couldn't he be brave too?

"I hate leaving the children alone," Mom said, "but our friends with the Border Patrol will stop to make sure everything's okay."

"I ain't scared," Hank said.

"The kids will be fine," Dad said. "Do you have a sleeping bag, Hank?"

Grady looked at Hank, hoping he'd say yes. He wouldn't be as scared if Hank were there.

"Sure, I got a sleeping bag," Hank said.

"Why not stay here tonight?" Mom said. "Save you some time in the morning."

"Then it's settled," Jeb said. "I'm mighty grateful to you."

Grady thought his excitement would keep him awake that night. But he slept soundly as usual.

The next morning everyone helped load limes onto *The Banana Boat*. Afterward both their parents repeated instructions they'd discussed the night before.

"For gosh sakes," Grady said, corking his fear. "You're only going for a day and a half."

"Still, you kids remember what we've talked about," Dad said. He started the motor and cast the stern line. Then he pointed the bow north.

Grady waved until his arm ached. Then he turned to Hank. "What shall we do first?" he asked.

As Hank had predicted, time passed much as time usually passed in the Keys. They went treasure hunting. And they brought back half a crate of oranges. Grady tried to write a poem while Hank drew a picture.

"You two should do a book," Maggie said. "Grady could write the words. Hank could draw the pictures. I'll be your business manager and make us all rich."

"Nice dream," Grady said.

Before supper time Ace and Lucky arrived. They were holding up crawfish tails. "We've brought supper," Ace called.

"Great," Grady said. "We love crawfish. And we can heat Mom's conch chowder too."

They cooked outside. They added oranges, bananas, and goat milk to the menu. Grady thought it was the best meal he had ever tasted.

Later Lucky played his harmonica. They sang "Row, Row, Row Your Boat" and "When the Saints Come Marching In."

When the sun began to set, Ace held his palm toward the sun. "About an hour until sunset."

"How can you tell?" Grady asked.

"I sight with my forefinger on the horizon. Then I count the number of fingers between the horizon and the bottom of the sun. Each finger equals 15 minutes. It's high time we headed home," he said.

Grady tried Ace's system of time telling. And it worked. Why, it was almost as good as having a wristwatch.

"You kids take care," Lucky said. "If anything scares you, slip out the back door. Hide in the thicket. Nobody will find you there."

Grady hated to see the men leave. But he corked the thought. Mope, he thought. Don't be a mope.

He and Maggie taught Hank to play Hearts. He couldn't imagine anyone not knowing that game. But Hank caught on quickly. At bedtime Maggie let the boys go to bed first.

Grady lay stiff with fear, listening to night sounds. Something splashed into the water. Goat's bell tinkled. He could hear Hank's quiet breathing. A pumpkin-orange moon rose behind the mangroves and shone through the window.

The next thing Grady knew, someone was shaking his shoulder. Then a hand clamped over his mouth. Maggie whispered into his ear.

"Wake up. Don't say a word. Don't make any noise," she whispered.

Grady brushed Maggie's hand away. All his fears

of being alone on Big Shark Key filled his head. He sat up and listened. "Someone's outside," Maggie said.

Grady slipped from under the mosquito netting and padded to the window. He saw nobody. Maggie took his hand, and they tiptoed to the kitchen.

They stood listening.

"I hear voices," Grady whispered. "Some are speaking English. Some are speaking another language. Maybe Spanish."

Grady peeked out the kitchen window. He saw a file of men heading toward their front door. He jumped as Hank suddenly tapped his shoulder. "What's up?" Hank said.

Grady let Hank look out the window. They saw the strangers creeping closer and closer. Goat bleated. The men stopped as if frozen in time. Then the leader motioned the others to wait while he walked on.

Grady felt Hank clinging to him. He tried to pull Hank toward the back door. But fear froze Hank to the spot. Someone had to be brave. If Hank wasn't going to be, then Grady guessed it would have to be him.

The man paused just outside the door. Grady fought the coppery taste at the back of his throat. He put on the brave face he had practiced so long. He would need it now more than ever. When they heard the stealthy turn of the doorknob, Grady had an idea.

"Dad! Dad!" Grady shouted. "I hear someone

outside. Come quick!"

"I'm scared." Hank said. He was shaking with fear.

Grady forced a low gruff voice and called out, "Go back to sleep. I'll get my shotgun and take a look outside."

Then Grady grabbed both Maggie and Hank. He hurried them out the back door and into the thicket.

They hid.

They listened.

They held their breath.

8

Journal in the Icebox

"Vamos! Vamos!"

Grady had seen enough Western matinees to know *vamos* meant "scram."

"What a good idea for letting them know someone was home!" Maggie whispered. "Grady, you really scared them away."

"Who were they?" Hank asked.

"Aliens," Grady said. "They had to be."

The kids heard a motor splutter to life then drone into the distance. They waited longer. Then Grady led them back into the house. Maggie lit the lantern.

"I'm staying up," Hank said. "I ain't scared, but I'm staying up until daylight."

Maggie winked at Grady. He felt the golden halo of her approval. Maybe there was a strong chance that he wasn't a mope—or a coward.

It was early afternoon the next day before their parents arrived home. Grady blurted their story. "I wrote it all down in my journal. You can read the details later," he said.

Grady looked at their boat. It looked as full now as it had been when they left. "Did we get rich selling limes?" he asked.

Mother laughed. "They paid us fairly. But we had to buy supplies and gasoline."

"We're holding our own," Dad said. "Sometimes what a person earns isn't as important as what he manages to save. I left a little money with your grandfather to keep for us."

Grady knew why Dad hadn't put the money in the bank. They had lost money when the government closed banks a few years ago. Dad didn't trust banks.

"What did you get?" Grady asked. He eyed the boxes in the boat.

"Fresh meat," Dad said. "And a block of ice that should last a day or two."

Mom smiled at Hank. "We brought you a carton of Ne-hi Cola. I think you and Grady finished the last one days ago."

Hank reached for the soda pop. "Thank you, Mrs. Cummings. Ne-hi Cola is the best thing I've ever tasted."

"We have another surprise," Dad said. "We've hired two men to help work the lime grove. And they'll arrive in about two weeks. They'll help dig the little lime shoots sprouting in the grove. Mr. Baxter will pay ten cents each for them."

"What about the men's families?" Grady asked. "Any kids?"

"They've moved in with relatives," Dad said. "We've brought tents for the men to live in. Rustic. But it'll be better than a hobo jungle in Miami. I can pay them when Mr. Baxter pays me. We'll still make a small profit. And we'll have helped two other families."

⚓ ⚓ ⚓ ⚓

The week passed quickly. Soon Jeb returned for Hank. A trip to the barber had tamed his hair and beard. And he smelled of Bay Rum lotion.

Jeb handed Hank a sack. "Brought you something," he said.

Hank pulled out a book. "Grady, look! A book about seabirds!" he exclaimed.

Grady stood closer. Together they looked at egrets, cormorants, and herons. Grady liked the smell of the ink and the slick feel of the paper.

"It's a swell book, Hank," Grady said.

"Maybe someday we'll have a book with our names on it," Hank said.

"Brought something else too," Jeb said. He pulled out a smaller sack.

When Hank peeked inside, he shouted. "Colored chalk! Grady, our book will be in color."

"And I brought you a new notebook to write in," Jeb said, handing Grady a book with gold-edged pages.

"Oh, thank you, Mr. Burltee! This is really great," Grady said, beaming.

"Hank, I hate to see you leave," Grady said. "We need to draw and write."

"We'll do it one day soon," Hank promised. "Nothing's going to change between us."

Hank was right. Nothing changed between them. They were friends. But other changes began to bother Grady in just a few days.

For one thing, the water teemed with fish. But

nobody could catch them. And Goat developed a huge appetite. They had to gather mangrove leaves to keep her fed.

"Grady," Mom said, "bring in some conchs, and I'll make more chowder."

Grady and Maggie swam to their usual conch spot. But they found no conchs. Grady swam another quarter mile and had to dive deep. Even so, he found only two conchs.

"It's like they're hiding from us, Maggie," Grady said.

The next day Jeb arrived in his skiff. His scowl warned Grady of bad news.

"Come to warn you," Jeb said. "There's going to be a big blow. All signs point to it."

"What signs?" Dad asked.

"Critter signs," Jeb answered. "Conchs hiding in deep water. Crawfish moving in the daylight instead of at night. Mosquitoes biting in daytime in spite of the wind. Storm's brewing. I've come to get water and to warn you."

Grady felt uneasy. Where had Jeb learned to forecast the weather? But what if he was right? Everyone helped Jeb fill his water bottles and carry them back to the skiff.

"I think we'll be safe here," Dad said. "The house is sturdy. We'll batten the hatches and sit out any blow that comes up."

"Would you and Hank like to stay here a day or two?" Mom asked.

Grady hoped Jeb would say yes.

"Thank ya kindly, ma'am. But Hank and I will be fine," Jeb said. "I've sailed plumb into the cove. We'll be protected. We've ridden out lots of storms together."

Even as Jeb left, the wind came up. The air grew more humid. They tied *The Banana Boat* to the mangrove trees. They covered the motor with heavy canvas.

"Everyone help me fix some extra food," Mom said.

But time ran out. In minutes a squall shook the house. They closed shutters. Rain poured down like emptying buckets. And Grady had never seen such wind. Boxes and crates flew through the air. Grady could only wonder what Hank was doing in all this wind.

The sound of Goat bleating mixed with the howling of the wind. It was a pitiful sound.

"Maggie, come help me bring Goat inside," Dad said. They went outside to rescue their pet and source of milk.

After only a couple of minutes, Maggie and Dad returned. They were leading Goat, who was shaking from being drenched and scared.

"Grady, get your journal. This is your chance to write about a hurricane," Maggie said as she grabbed a towel to dry her dripping hair.

"Is this really a hurricane?" Grady asked.

"I checked the wind gauge," Dad said. "It shows over 70 miles per hour. No time for writing. We're going to try to get some sleep. We'll need our energy later."

Grady felt fear growing like Gram's yeast bread. He didn't voice his fear. He pretended. Pretended bravery. Surely that's what the others were doing. Pretending.

"Will the water come inside the house?" he asked.

"If it does, we'll sit on the table," Dad said. "If it comes higher than that, we'll go into the thicket and tie ourselves high in sturdy trees."

"I think the gauge says 75," Maggie said. "That rain felt like needles hitting my eyeballs."

"Don't go out again, Maggie," Mom ordered. "You could blow away like a mangrove leaf."

"With no fish to eat, we'll have to ration our food," Dad said. "We don't know how long the storm will last. But let's count on two days." He set out crackers and a tin of beans for each day. Then added a banana for each of them.

"It's dark as night," Maggie said.

"It is night," Grady said. "Been night for two hours."

"Let's lie down," Dad said. "We must rest. We'll have lots of work to do when the storm ends."

"If we survive," Maggie said.

She's joking, Grady thought. She has to be joking. But he knew better. He had read about hurricanes.

Grady tried to think about other things. He remembered Hank's drawings that he had tucked into his journal for safekeeping.

"Grady," Dad called. "What are you doing up?"

"I'm putting my journal in the icebox," Grady shouted. "It's the only dry place I can think of."

Grady groped his way back to bed. He lay stiffly. He dangled one hand over the side of his mattress. If water came inside, he'd feel it and warn the others. He listened to the screaming wind. It was like a thousand conch horns all blowing at once.

Smells traveled with the hurricane. Grady smelled Goat. He inhaled the salty dankness of the night air. He smelled decaying seaweed and dead fish.

"Dad, will Hank's sailboat really stay afloat in this storm?" Grady asked.

"Jeb thinks it will," Dad answered. "Now go to sleep."

After the sky lightened in the morning, Grady knew he had slept. Where was everyone? He crept to the kitchen and found the family sitting around the table. He started to join them. But before he reached the table, he heard a terrifying ripping sound as his mother shouted.

"The roof! We're losing the roof!"

9

No Signal, Just Silence

They stared at a hole the size of a truck bed right over the kitchen table. Water pelted onto the oilcloth cover. Grady helped Dad drag the table aside.

"Now what?" Grady asked.

"We wait it out," Dad said. "Can't do repairs in this blow." He headed for the door.

"Where are you going?" Mom asked. "Please, Frank. Don't go outside."

Dad tied a line around his waist. "I'll tie the other end to a board on the house. I won't blow away. I want to see if our boat's still there."

Grady saw the rope grow tight moments after Dad disappeared into the storm. Had he fallen? What if he hit his head? What if . . .

It seemed like hours before Dad returned. Water streamed from his hair and into his eyes. He rubbed it off with the back of his hand.

"Wind speed over a hundred," Dad said. "Boat's okay. But the skiff's sunk. Maybe we can raise it later."

More pieces of roof blew away. At last they sat in a shell of a house with only sky overhead. Then suddenly, the storm stopped. Grady headed for the door.

"Wait," Dad said. "This may be the eye of the storm. The wind will change direction and blow as hard as before."

They waited. And waited. Dad's words came true. Wind and rain engulfed the island again. Grady watched water lap at their steps.

"I've got an idea," Grady said. "Let's prop two mattresses together like a tent."

"Good idea." Dad helped drag the mattresses from the beds. And it worked. At least they weren't getting quite so wet.

They spent another day watching it rain. They spent another night pretending to sleep—this time on the floor. Grady felt the boards move with the wind. It gave him a seasick feeling. And again he worried about Hank.

In the morning, the sun shone and the air smelled fresh. The storm had passed. Outside, Grady could hardly believe the damage. The mangroves stood leafless with limbs broken like matchsticks. The fruit trees looked like tall stumps. Their boat still floated. But most of the dock was gone. Tides had raised the skiff. Strangely, the oars were still in place.

"I'm going to signal Hank." Grady found his conch shell and blew a long blast.

They waited.

No reply.

"Hank's probably helping Jeb get the boat back in order," Dad said. "Can't expect him to be signaling you just yet."

But that's what Grady expected. He blew another blast. And another. And another. No response.

They were watching Dad try to start *The Banana Boat* when they saw Jeb in the distance. Walking, he splashed toward them in the shoreline shallows. Where was Hank? Jeb was alone.

Dad and Grady rushed to Jeb, offering support. He shook them off as if they were pesky mosquitoes.

"The Neptune," Dad said. "She went down?"

Jeb shook his head. And Grady knew something worse had happened. Something inside him curled up and died. He clapped his hands over his ears, refusing to listen.

Jeb wiped his nose on his shirtsleeve. Then he cleared his throat. "Hank's gone," he said.

Grady smiled with relief. Hank was just lost. "Then we'll help you find him, Jeb. We'll all help," he said.

Jeb shook his head. His glazed eyes told Grady that Jeb was looking right through him—maybe to someplace nobody else could see.

"Hank is . . . dead."

Grady felt as if an icy wind had frozen him. Jeb must have made a mistake. A dreadful mistake. Surely any minute now Hank would come splashing their way. You mopes! Scared you, didn't I? He could almost hear Hank's taunt floating from a distance.

But Hank didn't appear.

"Come to the house, Jeb," Mom said. "Let's sit down. Start at the beginning and tell us what happened. Maybe you're mistaken."

That's it, Grady thought. A big mistake.

Jeb followed Anna as if in a trance. At the house they sat on wet kitchen benches. Once Jeb began talking, he was like a motor with no off switch. Grady wanted to cover his ears. But he knew he didn't dare.

"Hank and I holed up in the cabin below deck

while *The Neptune* pitched and rolled. We both felt sick," Jeb said. "On the second morning Hank climbed the companionway for a breath of fresh air. I allowed it. I let him do it because I wanted to do the same thing. I caused his death. It was my fault. All mine."

"Don't blame yourself," Mom said. "This is no time to be placing blame."

"It was my fault," Jeb said. "Hank stuck his head into the storm. Right at that minute a piece of iron rigging broke loose from a mast. It hit him on the temple." Jeb talked through his tears. "He died instantly. No breath. No heartbeat. Gone.

"I pulled him into the cabin," Jeb said. "Thought maybe I could revive him. But no. It was no use." Jeb buried his head in his hands. His shoulders heaved with his sobs.

Grady wanted to say something to make Jeb feel better. But he couldn't speak. His voice was gone. Lost behind a great sadness. Maybe he would never talk again.

Dad patted Jeb on the shoulder. His voice shook. "We're so terribly sorry, Jeb. So terribly sorry. We'll help you make burial arrangements."

"Done that," Jeb said. "It's a Burltee tradition to be buried at sea. I wrapped Hank's body in a fresh sail canvas. I committed him to the water during the eye of the storm. In my fashion, I said a prayer. It was the best

I could do. He was all I had. And I want you, our only friends, to understand."

Grady wanted to shout "no." He wanted to set time back to days when he and Hank had been happy together. Swimming. Playing. Planning a book.

"Stay here with us," Mom invited.

"Thank you kindly," Jeb said, "but I need to be alone."

Grady understood. He needed to be alone too. He needed space for his heart to break. He started to leave the kitchen.

"Wait, Grady," Jeb said. "Hank had something he wanted you to have. He was going to give it to you after the storm was over." Jeb pulled a packet wrapped in plastic from under his shirt. "Please open it after I leave."

Grady took the packet. He ran to his room and flopped onto a sodden mattress. Hank. Hank. If only Hank had stayed with them during the storm. Grady drifted into another world.

"Grady. Grady. Wake up!" Mom shook his shoulder.

It was just a dream! Hank wasn't really gone! Grady started to smile, but then Mom continued.

"You've slept a whole day and night," she said. "We're getting ready to go home. I know you miss Hank. We all miss him. But we must go."

10
A Part of the Greatness

Grady sat up. "I'm afraid. I'm afraid for Hank. I'm afraid of being without Hank. There's nobody in this world to take his place. And what will he do without me?" Grady asked.

"I know, honey. But you're not feeling sorry for Hank," Mom said. "You're feeling sorry for Grady Cummings. You're feeling sorry for yourself. What would Hank think of that? He might call you a mope."

"And he might be right," Grady said. He reached for his mother's hand and managed to stand.

"Are you going to open the packet Jeb brought?" Mom asked.

"Maybe later," Grady said. "I can't open it yet. Where's my journal? I want it in my hand all the way home."

Grady couldn't eat breakfast. Nothing mattered now except Hank. He held his journal and Hank's packet on his lap while he pretended to eat. "Dad, what's going to happen to us now? Where are we going?" he asked.

"We'll stay with my folks for a while," Dad said. "But we have to leave here. There's no way I can build a new roof. The hurricane destroyed the lime grove. Mr. Baxter asked the Border Patrol to check on us. He's asked that we return to Miami. He'll help us out financially for a few weeks."

"What about your diamond stickpin?" Grady asked. "Will you have to sell it?"

"Forget that pin," Dad said. "I had a jeweler look at it when we were in Miami. It's a fine keepsake. But it's glass. Not a diamond."

Grady was sorry he had asked about the pin.

"Jeb's asked us to stop at Hidden Cove before we leave," Mom said. "He wants to gather at the place where he buried Hank and hold a brief farewell service."

"A funeral?" Grady thought he couldn't bear it.

"Let's call it a memorial service," Mom said.

Grady wanted no part of it. How could he stand it! But how could he refuse to attend? He opened the package containing his things and pulled out his spelling award.

Turning it over, he copied a haiku he had been working on for a long time. It didn't fit into the book he and Hank had planned. But now he knew what to do with it.

At the beach, Grady saw Goat in the boat. The hurricane had destroyed her crate. Would they have to travel clear to Miami with Goat loose in the boat?

"Jeb's going to keep Goat," Dad said. "Claims he's always needed a good milk goat."

When they reached Hidden Cove, Jeb waved to them from *The Neptune*. There was no room for him in their boat. So he invited them to his deck. For a moment Grady felt proud because he had climbed the rope ladder quicker than the others. Then he felt guilty. How dare he use any part of Hank's death to make himself feel proud!

After they sailed to Jeb's chosen spot, Jeb spoke.

"My grandpap was a minister. Some of his church words are in my mind." Jeb bowed his head. "For all things there's a season. A season to be born. A season to die. A season to love. A season to grieve. So be it. May the Lord have mercy on Hank's soul. Amen."

Jeb's words comforted Grady. He thought Hank would have liked them too. Then his mother began singing.

"Oh, when the saints come marching in . . ."

Jeb joined her. Their voices blended in the tradewind.

"Oh, when the saints come marching in."

Then everyone sang along. Grady thought they sounded like a real choir. He pulled out his spelling award. The sun glowed on the golden frame.

"Jeb, we have no flowers. But Hank liked this award. I'd like to leave it here," Grady said.

Mom touched his arm. "Read what you've written on it, Grady. Please."

Grady swallowed around his sadness. He pretended he was talking directly to Hank. And maybe he was. Who could say differently? He knew Hank would understand his words.

"This huge sea-sky world
Makes me proud to be a small
Part of the greatness."

Gently, he tossed the award into the sea. It floated like a golden flower.

"It was a lovely service, Jeb," Mom called to him. They had returned to their own boat and were preparing to leave.

Grady and Dad lifted Goat over the gunwale and lowered her gently into shallow water. Goat looked surprised. But she splashed toward the shore. Then they all waved as they headed north toward Miami.

Grady thought about Hank and about Jeb's words. Jeb named a lot of seasons. But he said nothing of the season his own grandfather had mentioned when they left Miami. A season of discovery.

Closing his eyes, Grady made a mental list of all his discoveries. Mangroves. Limes. Goat milk. Conch shell horns. Border Patrol. Turtles. Sponges. Aliens. Rumrunners. Hurricane winds.

Each new discovery led him to the biggest discovery of all—he had faced all those new things in spite of his fears. Bravery had been hidden deep inside himself. It was just waiting for him to discover it. That was a good thing to know.

Now Grady opened Hank's packet. He carefully protected it from the wind. Inside were bird sketches Hank had drawn. Great sketches. As good as any in Jeb's Key West bird book. When he pulled out the last sketch, he gasped.

"What is it?" Mom asked.

For a moment Grady couldn't speak.

"Why it's a picture of Hank himself," his mother said.

"He called it a self-portrait," Grady said. "He wanted me to trade my spelling award for it when he finished it. Oh, Mom!"

For the first time Grady sobbed. When he could speak again, he apologized.

"I'm sorry, Mom. I won't cry anymore," Grady said.

"It's okay, Grady. A person needs to get all the hurt out in the open where he can deal with it," Mom said.

Deal with the hurt? How could he ever do that? In his mind he tried to write a haiku about Hank. But the words wouldn't come. He closed his eyes to think.

Maybe Hank's self-portrait should go on their book cover. Making a book would be a big project. And so would dealing with his feelings about Hank.

At last Grady opened his eyes. He squinted into the wind for a moment. Then he began making a list of important things to do once he reached home.

Keep my shoulders squared.
Keep my chin high.
Write a haiku for Hank.
Find another wall for my brave-and-famous men pictures.
Remember Hank and Big Shark Key forever.